Wanting a little black gerbil & Crocodile dog

GENE KEMP

Chantal Fouracre

Illustrated by Alison Forsythe

Specially produced by

MAMMOTH

for School Book Fairs Ltd

First published in Great Britain as two separate volumes:

Wanting A Little Black Gerbil
First published 1992 by William Heinemann Ltd
Text copyright © Gene Kemp and Chantal Fouracre 1992

Crocodile Dog
First published 1987 by William Heinemann Ltd
Published 1994 by Mammoth
Text copyright © Gene Kemp 1987

This edition illustrations copyright © Alison Forsythe 1995

This omnibus edition first published 1995 by Mammoth
an imprint of Reed International Books Ltd
Michelin House, 81 Fulham Road, London SW3 6RB
and Auckland, Melbourne, Singapore and Toronto

ISBN 0 7497 2676 8

A CIP catalogue record for this title
is available from the British Library

Printed and bound in Great Britain
by Cox & Wyman Ltd, Reading, Berkshire

CONTENTS

Chapter One

BEN RAN, JACKET flapping, feet flying, new trainers full of bounce. He jumped down the last four steps from their flat, pushed open the swing door that led to the back of the shop and ran in.

'Mum, can I go to the pet shop?'

His mother stopped filling the apple section.

'Yes, you can. But mind the road. Cross carefully.'

Ben shot through the Fruit and Vegetable shop, fizzing like a pop bottle, dodging all the customers.

'Watch it, lad,' shouted Mr Mackensie, the owner, so Ben slowed down.

Once through the door he sped off to the shops, the supermarket, bank, post office, butchers, bakers, hairdressers. Then to his favourite, the pet shop, on the other side, across the road which Ben's mother worried about.

'I'm all right on my own,' Ben always said.

And he was. He was used to it. There'd only ever been him and his Mum. But he didn't want her to worry, so he always crossed with the green man.

The pet shop was busy. Ben elbowed his way through, past the tropical fish to the back of the shop where his favourites were.

'What about my sausages, then?' squawked a loud, rusty voice. Percy the parrot, older than anything, sat on his perch keeping an eye on things.

'Who's a pretty boy then?' he croaked, flapping his wings.

Ben picked up a bit of bark and held it close to him. Percy reached out, took it with his claw and put it into his wicked beak.

'Bye,' said Ben, moving on to the small cages standing in racks. Golden brown and white hamsters huddled, sleeping in three of them, and there were two cases of mice.

On the ground stood the bigger boxes with two rabbits and a guinea pig with crimpy fur. Two new cages stood on a higher shelf, and inside the cages five new furry animals.

Ben couldn't take his eyes off them. He'd never seen anything like them before. Bigger than mice, smaller than hamsters, balls of fluff with bright eyes and big back legs and tails, they were just great. Two were pale grey, two pure white and the other was smudgy black, a sooty ball of fur.

Ben put his little finger up to the bars of the cage. One of the little creatures scampered over and sniffed it, his nose wrinkling. With his other hand Ben scrabbled in his pocket. Surely he'd got some bits and pieces in there. Yip. A peanut. Quick as a flash he pushed it inside the

9

bars of the cage. The little black animal put out his paws, like two little hands, took the peanut, sat up on his hind legs and nibbled it.

When he'd finished he dropped down to four legs, turned and ran across the cage to the water bowl, back legs going thumpety thump, thumpety thump, thumpety thump.

Ben wanted that little black creature more than he'd wanted anything in the whole of his life. He stood there, watching it, its bright eyes, its fluffy fur, its little legs, its big tail. He was pleased that it had taken the nut and not been afraid of him.

'I want you, little black creature,' he whispered through the bars.

Slam! The door banged shut and a gang of noisy kids rushed through the shop. They pushed and shoved, nearly knocking Ben over, talking, yelling, laughing, arguing, as if he wasn't there. They swept Ben along with them until he ended up right at the back of the shop.

When he'd got back to the cage, the shop assistant was sticking a label on it.

NEW
COLOURED GERBILS
£5 each.

Ben's heart sank. He couldn't believe it. To get one he'd have to save for ages. He'd need lots of pocket money. He must manage somehow to find five pounds, BEFORE SOMEONE ELSE BOUGHT HIM.

At tea time he told his Mum all about the gerbil.

'You see, Mum, he's just perfect. All black and furry and clever. He'd be happy with me. I'd do all the cleaning out – honest!'

'It's not just that. There's the cage and the bedding and food as well as the gerbil. It's a bit much just now. We'll see about it later. Perhaps for your birthday . . .'

'But that's ages . . .'

'Ben, I can't manage it now. You'll have to be patient. I'm sorry,' said his mother. 'They'll have lots more gerbils in the shop.'

'But not that one. Not that little black gerbil.'

Ben choked back the tears.

That night in bed he thought about the little gerbil so hard and so long that as he drifted off to sleep he could feel the pitter patter of feet across the counterpane, a small furry creature curled up in the crook of his elbow.

He fell asleep trying out names.

'Smudge, or Blackie, or Jet. . . Whisper . . . or . . . Thumper . . . zz . . . zzz.'

Somehow or other he had to have that little black gerbil.

Chapter Two

'BEN BEAM! Lives in a dream!' called out Jimmy Todd and Kevin Spears as Ben made his way into school. He didn't hear them. Not even the school falling down could have stopped him daydreaming about the little black gerbil.

Ben imagined him tucked up in his pocket, the small warm body next to his side. He planned a day at school for a (special) black gerbil.

Before School

Smuggle gerbil into desk with bedding, food and water in a cut-off yoghurt cup.

After Assembly

Check on his safety. (He'd probably be curled up asleep in between his lunch box and pencil case!)

Playtime

Give him a run in the classroom. Simon and Penny (his friends) would be amazed at the trust the gerbil placed in him. Even Todd and Spears would shut up when he showed off his tricks!

He was planning to take his pet into "Singing Together" (tucked up in the end of his tie) when he bumped into Miss Tanner and knocked the pile of songbooks to the floor.

'Ben Beam! Wake up!' she exclaimed.

Ben mumbled sorry and picked up the books. Miss Tanner helped.

Together they made their way to the classroom.

The class were doing a Project on Animals. They'd made folders on horses, cats, dogs, monkeys, elephants, tigers and all endangered species, even sharks and poisonous jellyfish. Art was Ben's favourite subject, and he'd begun a big picture of a lion. But he left it and started a new picture, a picture of a little black gerbil.

'Hiya!' said Simon, who sat next to him. Ben took no notice.

'Hey! Guess what . . .' Simon began again.

'QUIET,' said Miss Tanner, trying to take the register.

'I've got a rabbit!' hissed Simon. 'Dad bought it!'

Ben's happy dream-bubble burst. Why should Simon have a rabbit? It wasn't fair!

Even if he saved every penny he got, it would take weeks before he could buy the gerbil. By then it would have gone for sure. While Simon had his rabbit.

Ben hated Simon. And his rabbit.

It was a long, draggy day. Simon told everyone over and over again about the rabbit. A crowd of kids was going round to see it after

school and Ben was also invited but he invented an excuse and ran out on his own.

Quicker than quick, he rushed to the pet shop, scared stiff that the gerbil might already have been sold. As he went he sang under his breath,

'If I don't . . . tread on the cracks . . . he'll be there . . . he'll be there . . . he'll be there.'

Vroom! In at the door of the pet shop straight into a stomach with a very fat man behind it.

'Look where you're going!' the man cried.

But Ben only had eyes for THE CAGE. Was he there or had somebody bought him? He couldn't see him. He must have gone! Oh, no! PANIC! PANIC!

But there he was. Black, furry, fantastic! Suddenly he stretched up on his back legs like a tiny kangaroo. Ben loved him, wanted him as much as ever. He must have him for his own. All he needed was the money to buy him. But how was he to get five pounds? And the rest for the cage and a wheel, the bedding and the food. What Ben needed was to find treasure!

Thinking hard he wandered out of the door. Treasure troves didn't seem likely but he could do jobs for people. And he'd save his pocket money, to add to what there was in his money box. If he didn't tread on the cracks in the pavement it would be all right, he'd get enough money. He bounced along the pavement dodging the cracks.

Something gleamed in one of those cracks, something round, something bright and shiny.

Ben bent down to pick it up.

Treasure!

A beautiful new pound coin. He looked round. No one was near him. No one was looking for a pound coin on the pavement.

'I think I can keep it,' thought Ben and he put it in his pocket.

'Hey, that's mine. Hand it over, it's all I've got till next week.' A mum with a double buggy popped out of nowhere holding out her hand. For a minute Ben thought of running away. Then slowly, with a deep sigh, he gave her the coin.

All the way home he went on looking in the pavement cracks, but all he found was a lolly stick and a safety pin.

Chapter Three

AND WHO SHOULD be waiting at home but his Grandma.

'Got any jobs for me?' he burst out, panting hard, not even saying 'Hello.'

'I ... don't ... know, Ben,' she answered, surprised. 'Why? Is it Job Week or something?'

'No, it's just that I want to buy a little black gerbil. And Mum says we haven't got 'nuff money 'cause of the bills and everything.'

'Well ... you can go and fetch me the evening paper. And some peppermints. You know the ones I like. Here's the money.'

'Goodness me. Did you go by space shuttle?' Grandma asked five minutes later, but Ben was panting too hard to answer. Gran took the paper and peppermints from him and handed

18

over some coins. 'Here. This'll help towards whatever it is you want.'

Ben ran to his bedroom and counted up his money. It still wasn't enough.

He bounced round next door and rang the bell and Mrs Crockett answered, a big lady, rather grand but always kind to Ben.

'Any jobs?' he asked. 'Please,' he added. He'd done jobs for her before. She couldn't let him down this time, could she?

'All right. I'm sorting out rubbish in the kitchen. Bottles go here for the bottle bank. The newspapers in a pile here for recycling. The rest go in this bag. I've been turning out my son's room. He's grown-up now and getting rid of all his old stuff. You can have those comics if you like.'

'Oh, great,' said Ben, but he was *really* looking to see if there was anything for a little black gerbil.

His eyes were so busy searching that they didn't see an old tin of paint which hadn't got its lid on properly. Ben knocked it over and it rolled. Out oozed squelchy dirty-white paint all over the rubbish and onto the kitchen floor.

'Oh, Ben!' said Mrs Crockett, then, 'No, don't worry, you couldn't help it. Never mind, I'll finish off here.'

'Wait,' said Mrs Crockett.

Ben waited.

'What about this? I think it's too good to throw away, but my son doesn't want it any more. Would you like it?'

IT was a large cage with little stairs leading to *two* upstairs rooms, a wheel and two little bowls. An unused packet of pet food stood inside it.

'Would I like it?' Ben cried. 'You can bet your life I'd like it.'

'Yippee!' he shouted as he carried the cage home. 'All I need now is THE LITTLE BLACK GERBIL!'

Chapter Four

NEXT DAY, AFTER school dinner, Ben hurried back to his classroom to finish his gerbil picture. It was on Miss Tanner's desk. Next to it stood two untidy piles of exercise books and lying between them like a little animal lay a fat leather purse. It was open and Ben found he was looking at a five pound note.

'Gerbil money,' he thought and the little black creature danced round and round in his head.

Footsteps ran up behind him and faster than a streaky fox Jimmy Todd popped up at his side.

'Naughty, naughty! Teachers shouldn't leave money lying around,' he grinned. 'We'd better put it into her bag.'

Jimmy's fingers were quick and nimble.

'There – that's it,' he said and shot away.

Ben tidied up the books, picked up his picture and went to his desk. He would never really have taken the money, however much he wanted the little black gerbil.

Miss Tanner was pleased that he'd tidied up the books for her.

'I was in such a rush. Thank you, Ben.'

Miss Tanner told her class she was pleased with them.

Later she told them she was not pleased with them and had another talk, this time about

respecting other people's property, and how wrong it was to steal.

You see, the five pound note had gone. It wasn't in the fat leather purse any more.

'We didn't take it, Miss,' said Simon.

'It was with the books, I know,' said a sad Miss Tanner to the Headmaster, who had arrived. 'I had to rush off and leave it all for a minute,' she added.

'Miss, Ben Beam tidied your books,' said Jimmy Todd.

'Oh, Ben!' said Miss Tanner.

Ben jumped up. 'It wasn't me. It wasn't!'

'Ben wouldn't do a thing like that!' shouted Simon.

'QUIET! Come with me, Ben. We'll talk about it in my office,' said the Headmaster.

Ben stumbled out of the classroom past all the staring faces. He wanted to cry. He felt awful.

At the end of school time, a subdued Ben walked home. He didn't want to go to the pet shop or even think about his gerbil. The awful events of the day still crowded in his head. The terrible unfairness of it all. He hadn't stolen the money. What was the point of wanting his little black gerbil when everything was against him, when everything went wrong?

He couldn't forget how the Headmaster had spoken about truth and honesty, about not stealing things and all the time he, Ben, *was* telling the truth!

It was the school caretaker who saved the day. Luckily for Ben he'd been cleaning the windows and he had seen another lad at the teacher's desk, touching things. That red-haired one, Johnny? or Jimmy? he explained. He knew Ben hadn't taken the note.

Ben was glad that the caretaker had seen, and glad that Sir made Jimmy confess. And the five pound note turned up in an exercise book where Jimmy had put it for fun!

Chapter Five

WHEN BEN REACHED home he felt too tired to bother with anything much. He just wanted his bed, his books and toys, his own safe room around him. He lay down, his face buried in his pillow. 'Where have the happy times gone?' he thought to himself and then, 'Do I even want the little black gerbil? *Really* want him like before?' He pictured the little creature, its brightness and alertness stirring him. Suddenly Ben knew that he had to see him again.

'Even if I can't buy him, I can still see him each day at the shop!' he thought, and he tipped his money onto the bed, scooped it up and ran out of his room and into the street.

'Watch out, Ben!' gasped Grandma as Ben

bumped into her and fell down. She helped him up and hugged him.

'Grandma,' said Ben, quietly.

She looked at him closely. 'You look a bit pale and worn out. Here, have a bit of extra pocket money to cheer you up,' and she gave Ben a one pound coin.

For Ben, the sun shone again. 'Thank you, Grandma, so much,' he said and hugged her hard.

He could buy the gerbil. Hip hip hip hooray. He could buy it today. Today was Gerbil Day!

'Here I come,' he thought, running into the pet shop and straight to the cage.

His heart stopped. The cage was empty.

It was quite bare. The little black gerbil had gone. All the gerbils had gone.

Chapter Six

'I'M WORRIED ABOUT Ben,' said his Mum to Miss Tanner.

'Why, what's the matter? Is he ill or something?'

'No, he's not ill. But he's got no interest in anything at all. As soon as he comes home from school he goes and lies on the bed. It's not like him at all. I'll have to take him to the doctor.'

But the doctor said there was nothing wrong with Ben.

One day, Ben started helping at the pet shop. When he'd finished he asked Mr Biddle if he'd got any more gerbils coming in.

'Not at the moment,' said Mr Biddle. 'But if you come in and help me now and then you'll be able to keep your eyes open for them, won't you?'

So Ben did. Almost every afternoon he went and helped at the pet shop. Sometimes gerbils appeared in the cages but never a black one. The end of term came and school finished. Ben enjoyed being with the animals. The hamsters and mice grew to know and trust him. They didn't scuttle away when Ben cleared out their cages, but snuffled up to his hand and took treats from him.

Mr Biddle liked to have Ben helping him and said that the world needed more people like him caring for animals unselfishly.

One evening, at the start of the holidays, Mr Biddle seemed sad. When Ben asked why, he took him to the back corner, and there curled up in an open topped box was the smallest baby gerbil Ben had ever seen – all alone lying still, eyes closed, its soft black downy fur just growing.

'A friend brought him in today,' he said. 'A cat got the mother and the others. But I haven't time to feed him every two hours, that's the trouble.'

'I have,' said Ben. 'I've got time.'

Mr Biddle smiled. 'Come on, then. I'll show you what to do, lad. Keep the box in a warm spot and feed him every two to three hours in the daytime. At night one feed will do. Will your mother let you feed him at night?'

'I'll keep him in the bedroom,' said Ben.

Mr Biddle showed Ben how to feed the little creature with a dispenser for putting drops into sore ears.

'If you save this one you can have him,' he said. 'But you mustn't mind if he dies. Sometimes they do, you know.'

'Not this one,' thought Ben as he left the shop, holding the box with extra special care.

At home he held out the box for his Mum to see.

'Poor little thing,' she said.

The little black gerbil lay there, hardly breathing.

'We'll try,' she said.

But it seemed as if trying wasn't enough. The little black gerbil would not drink the milk.

'It's too small to live,' thought Ben. 'Oh, little gerbil, please don't die.' He watched the creature closely. Noticed its tiny sealed eyes, its fragile naked limbs and small curled round body showing pinky-blue through the fur. Tears trickled down Ben's face. 'Keep breathing, keep breathing,' he thought.

Suddenly he had an idea. He knew baby puppies liked warmth and security.

'Mum! Let's warm him up with a hot water bottle!' he cried.

Quickly his Mum fetched a hot water bottle with a furry cover. Ben made a hollow in it with his fist and they laid the little creature in it. After a moment the gerbil wriggled and feebly kicked its legs. It liked the fur and the warmth.

'Try now!' said Mum.

Carefully Ben pushed the feeder into the tiny mouth and squeezed a drop. Amazingly the gerbil swallowed, its mouth and throat muscles working. Ben did it again, and again the milk went down. Ben smiled.

Two hours later Ben fed him again and again, and then again and again, and each time the little black gerbil DRANK SOME MORE!

At last his Mum sent him to bed. But it was difficult to get to sleep. Would the little black gerbil still be alive in the morning? Would he be there for Ben to talk to, to hold, to watch, to feed each day when he came home from school?

Chapter Seven

BEN RUNS, JACKET flapping, feet flying, new trainers full of bounce. He pushes open the swing door and springs up the stairs two at a time.

He runs into the flat and into his own room where a cage stands on his chest of drawers.

'Tch ... tch ... tch,' calls Ben in their secret language.

'Tch ... tch,' and from the nest box out wriggles a furry black gerbil. With bright beady eyes looking at Ben, he runs thumpety, thumpety across the cage and in a moment boy and gerbil are playing happily.

Just as always the little gerbil runs up Ben's arm and sits on his shoulder where he scutches his fur up and waits. Just as always Ben gives him a peanut and, balancing on back legs, he holds it in his front paws to eat it.

He is just a little black gerbil after all. Just a little black furry animal that belongs to a boy.

Chapter One

'IT DOESN'T LOOK like a nice dog,' I said.

My sister Agg, known as The Agg, came through the doorway with this dog on a long piece of string. Then she said at the top of her voice (and she's got a voice like a fire engine siren, dar-da, dar-da, you know what I mean),

'He's lost. So I brought him home with me. He's a nice dog.'

I looked at it and it looked at me.

It was long, and low on the ground with short hairy legs, a coat like a coconut and a long, thin, ratty tail. Nearly worst of all were its little mean eyes, one brown, the other blue. But really worst of all was its great long snout-face full of teeth, hundreds of them – sharp, pointed teeth.

It lifted up its snout-face and snarled at me.
I jumped back, being chicken by nature. This
dog would make anyone chicken.

'Don't be stupid,' shouted The Agg. 'You
can see he's a nice dog.'

The Agg is the bossiest person I know. She's
a walking laser beam, nine foot high and she's
only ten. I think she'll grow up to be a giantess.
Sometimes I've wondered if she's an alien from
outer space dropped here by accident or
through some Great Plan of the Universe.

She's got this big swinging plait she uses to

knock me out. And she's the best footballer in the school. I ask you.

Once I asked my mother if she was adopted but she said, 'Of course not. Whatever made you think that? Mary's your very own sister.' Mary's her real name. But Dad calls her Agatha Gripper, so we all call her The Agg.

I'm Gregory, but they all call me The Splodge. I've got a patch over one eye to stop me squinting and whenever I try to take it off for a minute The Agg tells on me, mean pig.

But back to *that dog*. The Agg picked it up and cuddled it. She wants to be a lion tamer when she grows up. I mean when she grows old. She's up high enough, already. And I'll say that for her. She must have nerves of steel. She pushed her face right into that snouty face with all those teeth and sang to it, 'Diddums a lovely dog then, diddums, diddums, diddums . . .'

It was really yucky.

'See how miserable he is,' she shouted at me. 'He's a stray. And he's been ill-treated. You can always tell.'

'It would be hard to ill-treat that dog. It would have your hand off if you tried anything.'

'Look. See how neglected he is. He needs love and attention.'

She seized my hand and pushed it against his dirty coat. I jumped back.

'Poor thing,' cried The Agg. 'He's starving.'

'That's no reason for it to eat me.'

I backed right up against the television, hands tucked behind me.

'I'm gonna ask Mum if I can keep him. Where is she?'

'Gone shopping. With Flossie.'

Flossie is our old fat spaniel, kind and comfortable and dead lazy. When she goes for a walk she sits down every three minutes.

'Mum won't let you keep it. And what about

Flossie? And the cat? They won't want a crocodile – I mean a dog like *that* about the place. And it might kill the mice in the shed. And the tortoise.'

'Rubbish,' bawled The Agg. 'They'll love him.'

'Look,' I said desperately. 'It must belong to somebody and they're probably looking for it right now. Missing it. Even crying for it.'

It didn't seem likely. I thought the owner was probably emigrating to Australia. But I kept going.

'Suppose you take it back to where you found it? Then someone might come for it.'

She stuck out her lips at me like she does when she's mad.

'He's mine now,' she said through her teeth, while the crocodile growled through his, 'and no one is going to take him away from me.'

'I tell you this,' and I knew it was a wally thing to say even as I said it, 'if that dog stays I'm leaving.'

'Good. I'll pack your case for you,' said The Agg.

The crocodile dog stayed of course.

And she called it Laddie.

Chapter Two

DAD SAID HE thought the dog was the nastiest thing he'd ever laid eyes on and he'd seen a few in his time. Mum said we must put an ad.

in the paper in the Lost and Found Column. Then the owners would claim it. 'They must be missing it,' she said.

'I shouldn't think so,' Dad said.

Mum put out a bowl of food for it as well as for Flossie, and Zebra the cat. It tried to eat the cat's food, got its nose scratched, wolfed down Flossie's and finally ate its own while the cat sulked.

'If we put it outside it might run back to its real home,' I said hopefully.

'Good idea,' Dad said.

'I think you're beastly and horrible, horrible and beastly,' howled The Agg. 'This is his real home. Can't you see he's been with people who haven't loved him?'

'I'm not surprised,' said Dad, opening the door, putting it out, and getting his foot bitten. Fortunately he was wearing leather boots. He didn't let The Agg open the door for an hour. She shouted dreadfully, though not loud enough to drown the howling going on outside in the garden.

Three people rang up to complain about the noise and both next door neighbours came to the kitchen door to ask if we'd gone mad and what we were going to do about the zoo at the front.

Suddenly the crocodile dog bounded in, quite unaware of the trouble it was causing. With a happy grin showing all its hundreds of teeth it

made a beeline for The Agg and put its head on her lap. She crouched over it making little whimpering noises. Flossie glared from the sofa and the cat sulked on top of the cupboard.

'I'll take it to the Police Station,' said Dad.

'The RSPCA would be better,' said Mum.

The Agg wailed. The dog snuggled closer to her.

'But it's a bit late,' Mum went on. 'It's probably closed by now.'

'Oh, it can stay tonight, then,' groaned Dad. 'As long as it's quiet. But only for tonight, mind.'

Chapter Three

I SUPPOSE I knew all along that it would stay. Whatever The Agg wants, The Agg gets. Mum put an ad. in the paper. No one came. Dad walked it all round the place where The Agg had first found it. No good. No one wanted to know.

One evening when she was at her music lesson, I bravely put on its lead, which The Agg had bought with her own money. I took it to the park and then I let it go and ran home, but it was no good. It got back before me.

'It used to be so peaceful before that dog came,' said Mum at breakfast one morning. She'd had to apologise to the next-door neighbour. Their cat had been stuck on the roof all night, chased there by Laddie. It was still dark when the fire brigade arrived to get it down.

'It's not his fault,' cried The Agg. 'Things annoy him.'

'I'll annoy him if he doesn't mend his ways,' said Dad. 'He might just end up in a Dogs' Home for Bad Animals. Or even in a cat food tin.'

You should've heard The Agg. She howled and cried and stamped her feet, tears spouting everywhere like fountains. So I went to school where it seemed quite peaceful after home.

Mr Clark is our teacher. He's all right, though he has got a temper. My friends there are Pete, and Jackie Brown, who's a girl but OK otherwise. There's a big kid there with red

hair called Foxy Lewis and you have to look out for him. He gets black moods and then . . . TROUBLE!

The morning was fine. We did some Maths. I wrote a story. We had Science and I did some work on my Space Project. After dinner we changed into our kit because it was football first of all. We picked teams and began to play. The sun was shining. For the first time ever I shot a goal. Then I shot another goal.

I felt absolutely brill. What a wonderful world.

'Dead lucky you are,' came Foxy Lewis's sneery voice right behind me. 'Or else you cheat.' He tried to trip me up but I whipped out of the way.

It was Foxy who fell in the mud.

'Stop messing about, Lewis,' cried Sir.

I felt even greater as we started up once more.

I ran down the pitch dribbling the ball and it was with me all the way until . . .

'What's that animal doing here? Get it off the pitch,' shouted Mr Clark.

I shot and missed. The whistle blew.

'Offside,' shouted Mr Clark. 'And somebody get rid of that dog before it ruins the game.'

I turned from the goal. In the middle of the

pitch a whirlpool raced at fantastic speed, a flying, barking, snapping whirlpool with a long thin ratty tail attached to it.

'Get out of here,' Sir was shouting, trying to send the whirlpool to the other side of the field. It swirled up and round and over him.

'Ouch, you beast. That was me,' Sir cried.

'It's a mad dog.'

'I'll get it for you, Sir.'

'Look out, it bites!'

'Look at all those teeth!'

'It's Splodge's dog!'

'No, it's not! It's my sister's.'

'I don't care whose dog it is. Just send it off!'

The game had stopped, everything in chaos, as Laddie the crocodile dog whirled up and down, round and round, snapping at the ball and the players and the goal posts and Sir.

Sir was trying to get the dog collar to hold it, when suddenly he slipped in the mud and fell, banging his head on the goal post. He lay on the ground absolutely still.

There were screams and shouts.

It seemed like the end of the world.

'You've killed him,' said Foxy Lewis to me.

'Fetch an ambulance.'

'Is he dead?'

'Fetch the Head teacher.'

'Fetch Splodge's sister.'

Children bent over Mr Clark. Somebody was crying.

'It's all your fault,' Foxy Lewis said to me.

And in the middle of all this the crocodile dog still ran up and down, round and round, lifting its nose in the air and snapping its hundreds of teeth.

I turned to fetch The Agg. It seemed to me she was the only one who could sort this lot out. But as I did, a figure appeared on the field. Mrs Parker, the Head teacher.

'Just you all stand still,' she said.

So we did.

Then she snapped her fingers at Laddie, the crocodile dog, and it ran over, tail down, stomach on the ground and lay at her feet, looking up at her in exactly the same way it looks at The Agg.

All was silent.

She ran over to Mr Clark, but he was already getting up to his feet, wobbling a bit, though. I was very glad to see he wasn't dead.

'Jackie Brown, you go inside with Mr Clark,' she said. 'Then someone can tell me what's happened.'

'It's all Splodge's fault,' said Foxy Lewis.

'Oh, no, it isn't,' I answered, managing not to cry.

'Well, you tell me about it anyway,' said Mrs Parker.

Chapter Four

SOME TIME LATER we sat in the classroom, silent and subdued. We'd changed out of our football kit and Mrs Parker had said a few words to us.

Mr Clark had gone home with concussion. Freddy, the caretaker, had arrived to put Laddie, the crocodile dog, in a shed. He said he wasn't doing this on his own, not with those teeth looking at him, thank you very much. So Mrs Parker sent for The Agg, who helped him imprison Laddie.

Then The Agg and me, we had to go to Mrs Parker's room where she told us that on no account was that dog to come to school, or enter the playground. She didn't wish to see it again, not ever. Even The Agg looked small when we came out together.

'Don't you dare say it's all my fault,' she hissed.

I didn't. I turned, put my tongue out at her and ran straight into the nit nurse. Of course I got told off again.

In the classroom a new teacher had arrived. Wow! I'd never seen anything like her. She'd got orange skirts down to her boots, and floating orange hair down to her waist, gynormous orange specs. Next to her, on the desk, sat a huge orange hat. She looked like a commercial for Eat More Fruit.

'D'you think she changes to green or red?' whispered my friend Pete.

'Hello, children,' she sang out. 'My name's Miss Elphick and we're going to have a simply super fun time.'

The class cheered up. This was certainly a change from Mr Clark. He didn't wear orange specs or talk about super fun times. Behind me I could hear Foxy Lewis making up rhymes for Elphick, and they weren't very nice.

'Children,' she cried again and her voice bounced off the walls and pinged in my head. We all waited.

'I want you all to *really* stretch.'

She reached up on tip toes stretching her arms wider and wider. It was amazing how wide she made herself.

'I'm filling the room,' she cried.

'She'll burst,' whispered my friend, Pete.

'Her or the walls,' said Foxy Lewis.

She sank down a bit then put a finger to her orange lips.

'I want you all to imagine you're tiny seeds! Now stand beside your chairs and bend down and curl up tight into a teeny weeny ball.'

There was a loud crash and a cry from Tony.

'I'm too big, Miss.'

'Of course you are, my dears,' pinged her

voice hitting several notes at once. 'I should have realised what fine big children you all are. Silly me. Now we'll push all these tables and chairs back against the walls and then we shall be free to MOVE AND GROW.'

We did.

'You,' she cried, pointing to Jackie, 'can run round and sprinkle rain on the seeds, so they start to grow.'

Jackie ran round and sprinkled.

We grew. I banged my head growing into a nearby table.

'Now I'm the SUN,' called out Miss Elphick.

'But you're a lady, Miss!'

'Not that sort of son! Just grow, grow, GROW!'

While we grew, she put on a tape.

'Grow to the music,' she cried.

A jar of flowers fell onto Tony as he grew to the music higher than anyone else.

'I'm soaking wet,' he bellowed.

'Never mind, boy. Just grow and grow. Enter into the spirit of Nature.'

We did. Plants grew and leapt and jumped around the room.

'Let it all happen!' trilled Miss Elphick.

And it did.

The door shot open and into the room flew a

long furry animal with teeth like a crocodile and a tail like a rat. Round and round it flew among the growing plants. Laddie, the crocodile dog had arrived to join in the super fun time.

Then everything went completely mad. Crocodile Dog headed straight for Foxy Lewis, every tooth glittering with menace. Foxy Lewis screamed and so did the rest of the class. Miss Elphick snatched her orange hat and charged after Crocodile Dog flapping it furiously.

'Owch,' shouted Foxy, nipped by Laddie and flipped by Miss Elphick's hat.

Later they said I was running away as I headed for the door to get out, but honestly, I thought the only thing to do was to fetch The Agg from the classroom next door.

'No, you don't. I'm coming too,' shouted Foxy, right behind me pursued by the crocodile dog being chased by Miss Elphick hitting him with her hat.

'He's getting me,' cried Foxy, just as Foxy got me, grab, and I fell splat, bang, crash . . . wallop.

Chapter Five

THE SCHOOL ORCHESTRA was playing bongo drums in my head, boom, boom, de da, boom, BOOM.

I opened my eyes on the wrecked classroom. Oh, no. Mrs Parker had once more arrived and everything, including time, had stopped except for the crocodile dog who lay quivering with love at her feet, and Jackie who was helping me to mine. As I stood up I could see, hanging from Laddie's teeth, a large piece of orange material.

Miss Elphick was wrapping round her all that remained of her floaty skirt.

The school orchestra stopped playing bongo drums in my head. Everything was quiet. Then Mrs Parker spoke.

'Jackie, you're a sensible girl. Take this animal to the caretaker and ask him to tie him up even more securely this time until Gregory and Mary can take him home.'

She looked very coldly at me and at the crocodile dog who drooped its tail and ears in sorrow.

Jackie went up to it and tried to pull it out of the classroom, but it wouldn't budge. Suddenly it ran to *me*! And lay at *my* feet!

'You'd better take him, Gregory. Jackie can go with you. The rest of us will . . . tidy up.'

Chapter Six

WE HURRIED OUT of the classroom at speed.
Jackie and me. I clutched the Crocodile Dog's
piece of string but stayed as far away from it as
possible.

None of it was fair. I hadn't done anything. I
didn't want the dog in the first place. I didn't
even like it. I hadn't brought it to school. I
couldn't help it if Mr Clark got splatted and
Miss Elphick was orange and nutty. I liked Mr
Clark and I'd rather have had football anytime.
Somewhere, something wasn't fair.

It was that rotten animal's fault.

I looked down at it and it looked up at me,
wagging its ratty tail.

'Come on, you,' I snapped, pulling the string
tightly (so that it hurt I hoped).

But it didn't come. Crocodile Dog had stopped and wouldn't move. Wouldn't budge.

Tug, tug, tug. But it lay low on its belly, back legs braced, ears a-prick, eyes shining bright, every tooth a-gleam, low rumbling growls coming from its throat.

'What's up?' asked Jackie.

'Nothing. It's just being stupid, that's all.'

'Grrrr! Grrrrh! Woof, woof, woof! Grrrh!'

'Oh, come on!'

It was no use. Crocodile Dog wouldn't go any further.

'What's got into you, you stupid animal?'

But Jackie had stopped dead too.

'Look! Look!' she cried, pointing at the cupboard beside us. Smoke was curling round the edges of the doors. Grey, wispy smoke. Very peculiar. I went to look at what was wrong.

'No, no, don't! Don't, Splodge!' shouted Jackie. 'Don't open those doors! The cupboard's on fire!'

Too late. Grabbing a handle, I had pulled the door open.

A lion's roar, a sheet of flame, a rumbling and a thundering, a fierce heat and a horrible scorching smell.

Jackie was shouting, 'Help, help. Ring the fire alarm!'

A huge fat cloud of smoke billowed all around us. My eyes streamed and I started to splutter and cough, throat burning. Jackie was screaming now.

'Fire! Fire! Help!'

Through the smoke loomed our caretaker, Freddy, then the buzzer sounded loud and terrifying, bells rang and there was the noise of running feet and people shouting. Then a voice sounding clear and calm.

'Walk steadily, children. Keep in line. Out of school into the playground. Steadily, there. Everything's all right.'

And all the school was trooped safely away from the smoke and the heat and the flames.

I was safe too. For the crocodile dog had seized me with its hundreds of teeth and dragged me to safety, ready to be lined up and checked from the registers, out there on the playground, clear away from the danger with all the other children.

Much later we sat in Mrs Parker's office, The Agg, Jackie, Crocodile Dog and me. I had one bandaged hand which hurt dreadfully and he was licking the other one.

'I'm just writing a note to your parents,' explained Mrs Parker, 'to let them know what

happened. And to say what a brave dog you've got there. A hero. With a bit more training he'll grow up into a very nice dog.'

'Yes, I know,' said The Agg. 'I always knew he was a nice dog.'

She and Mrs Parker smiled as if they understood one another perfectly. The mad idea came into my head that The Agg would end up just like her one day. But I didn't care. I put out my hand, very cautiously – because I did ache an awful lot – and stroked Laddie's head. For a moment I was afraid he was going to bite it but no, he just went on licking instead.

A Selected List of Fiction from Mammoth

The prices shown below were correct at the time of going to press.

☐	7497 1421 2	**Betsey Biggalow is Here!**	Malorie Blackman	£2.99
☐	7497 0366 0	**Dilly the Dinosaur**	Tony Bradman	£2.99
☐	7497 0137 4	**Flat Stanley**	Jeff Brown	£2.99
☐	7497 0983 9	**The Real Tilly Beany**	Annie Dalton	£2.99
☐	7497 0592 2	**The Peacock Garden**	Anita Desai	£2.99
☐	7497 0054 8	**My Naughty Little Sister**	Dorothy Edwards	£2.99
☐	7497 0723 2	**The Little Prince (colour ed.)**	A. Saint-Exupery	£3.99
☐	7497 0305 9	**Bill's New Frock**	Anne Fine	£2.99
☐	7497 1718 1	**My Grandmother's Stories**	Adèle Geras	£2.99
☐	7497 0041 6	**The Quiet Pirate**	Andrew Matthews	£2.99
☐	7497 1930 3	**The Jessame Stories**	Julia Jarman	£2.99
☐	7497 0420 9	**I Don't Want To!**	Bel Mooney	£2.99
☐	7497 1496 4	**Miss Bianca in the Orient**	Margery Sharp	£2.99
☐	7497 0048 3	**Friends and Brothers**	Dick King Smith	£2.99
☐	7497 0795 X	**Owl Who Was Afraid of the Dark**	Jill Tomlinson	£2.99
☐	7497 0915 4	**Little Red Fox Stories**	Alison Uttley	£2.99

All these books are available at your bookshop or newsagent, or can be ordered direct from the address below. Just tick the titles you want and fill in the form below.

Cash Sales Department, PO Box 5, Rushden, Northants NN10 6YX.
Fax: 01933 414047 : Phone: 01933 414000.

Please send cheque, payable to 'Reed Book Services Ltd.', or postal order for purchase price quoted and allow the following for postage and packing:

£1.00 for the first book, 50p for the second; **FREE POSTAGE AND PACKING FOR THREE BOOKS OR MORE PER ORDER.**

NAME (Block letters) ....

ADDRESS ....

....

☐ I enclose my remittance for ....

☐ I wish to pay by Access/Visa Card Number

Expiry Date

Signature ....

Please quote our reference: MAND